W9-AGQ-672

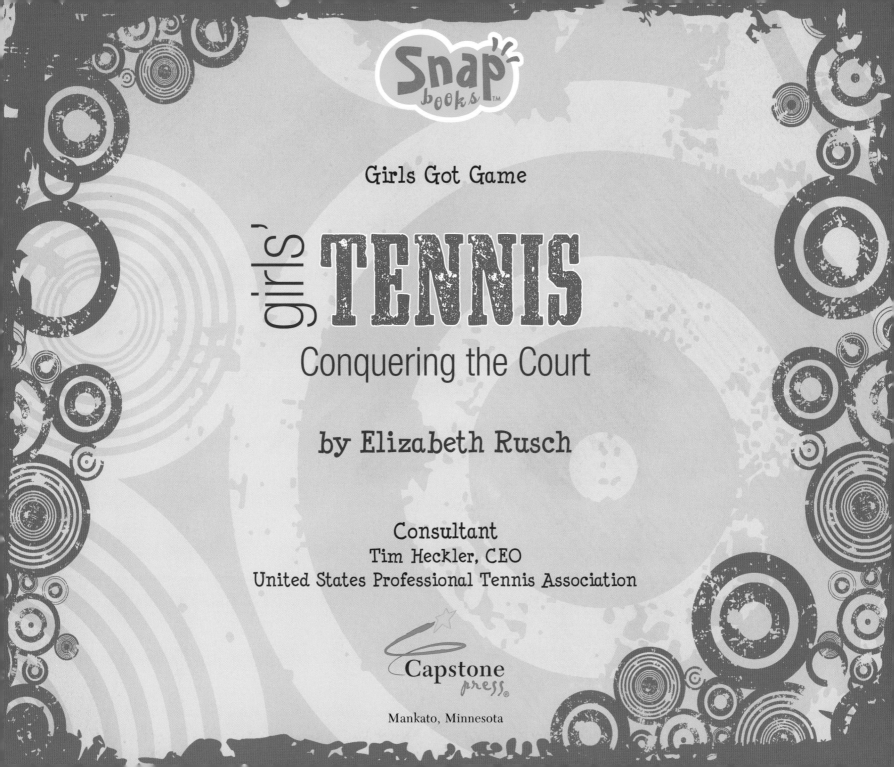

Girls Got Game

girls' TENNIS

Conquering the Court

by Elizabeth Rusch

Consultant
Tim Heckler, CEO
United States Professional Tennis Association

Capstone press®

Mankato, Minnesota

Snap Books are published by Capstone Press,
151 Good Counsel Drive, P.O. Box 669, Mankato, Minnesota 56002.
www.capstonepress.com

Library of Congress Cataloging-in-Publication Data
Rusch, Elizabeth.
    Girls' tennis: conquering the court / by Elizabeth Rusch.
    p. cm.—(Snap Books. Girls got game)
    Summary: "Describes tennis, the skills needed for it, and ways to
compete"—Provided by publisher.
    Includes bibliographical references and index.
    ISBN-13: 978-0-7368-6825-9 (hardcover)
    ISBN-10: 0-7368-6825-9 (hardcover)
    ISBN-13: 978-0-7368-9930-7 (softcover pbk.)
    ISBN-10: 0-7368-9930-8 (softcover pbk.)
    1. Tennis for girls—Juvenile literature. I. Title. II. Series.
GV1001.4.G57R87 2007
796.342082—dc22   2006021251

Editor: Amber Bannerman
Designer: Bobbi J. Wyss
Photo Researcher: Charlene Deyle
Illustrator: Kyle Grenz

Photo Credits: Capstone Press/Karon Dubke, 9, 12, 15, 19, 22, 23; Comstock
Klips, cover; Danielle Swope, 32; Getty Images Inc./Adam Pretty, 11; Getty
Images Inc./AFP/Adrian Dennis, 6, 25; Getty Images Inc./Alex Livesey, 28;
Getty Images Inc./Allsport/Chris Cole, 29; Getty Images Inc./Central Press/
Leonard Burt, 27; Getty Images Inc./Clive Brunskill, 5; Getty Images Inc./
Daniel Berehulak, 21; Getty Images Inc./Hulton Archive, 26; Getty Images
Inc./Jamie Squire, cover; Getty Images Inc./Matthew Stockman, 11
Heidi Miles, 17

1 2 3 4 5 6 12 11 10 09 08 07

TABLE OF CONTENTS

Chapter 1
QUEENS OF THE COURT 4

Chapter 2
SMASH SESSION 10

Chapter 3
GET IN THE GAME 16

Chapter 4
BECOMING A SMASH HIT 20

Chapter 5
PRO PLAYERS 26

Glossary 30

Fast Facts 30

Read More 31

Internet Sites 31

About the Author 32

Index 32

CHAPTER ONE

QUEENS OF THE COURT

What sport is dominated by powerful, graceful women? Tennis! Just look at who holds the most amazing records in tennis.

Martina Navratilova has the record for the most singles tournaments ever won, with 167 titles. And who is the reigning champion of Wimbledon? That's right, another woman. Billie Jean King's record of winning 20 Wimbledon titles has yet to be broken.

And a woman, Chris Evert, holds the best winning percentage in tennis pro history. Evert won 1,309 matches and only lost 146.

Women are the queens of the tennis court. But they weren't born royalty. They started right where you do, with a ball, a racket, and a love for competition. With lessons and lots of practice, maybe you can rule the court.

Tyra
Calderwood,
junior pro player

5

The Rules of the Court

So what kingdom do tennis players reign over? Courts, of course! Tennis courts can be made of cement, grass, carpet, or clay. They can be indoors or outdoors. A net separates the court into two sides.

In singles, it's just you face-to-face with your opponent. Your wits and skills are against hers. In doubles, two players on each side of the net work together to win. One player covers the right side of the court while the other covers the left. Or one player might protect the back of the court while the other protects the front.

Lindsay Davenport

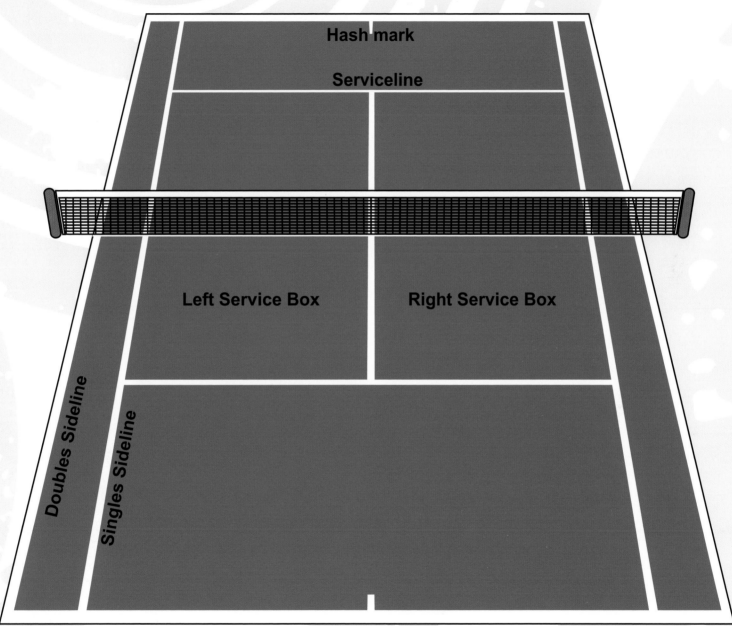

Hash mark

Serviceline

Left Service Box

Right Service Box

Doubles Sideline

Singles Sideline

Baseline

Game, Set, Match!

Hitting a tennis ball back and forth is a blast, but people who crave competition play matches. A tennis match is made up of points, games, and sets. Games start at zero or "love." One side must win four points, called 15, 30, 40, and game. The server calls out the score, with her score first.

If both sides get to 40, it's called deuce. If the serving side wins the point, they serve one more point called add-in. If they win this point, they win the game. But if they lose the point, the score goes back to deuce. Deuce can go back and forth for what seems like an eternity.

Hit a Winner

A player scores a point if she:

- Hits a good serve that the other player can't hit back. This is called an ace.
- Hits a ball in the court that the other player can't hit back. This is called a winner.

A player scores a point if the other player:

- Misses two serves in a row.
- Lets the ball bounce more than once before hitting it.
- Hits the ball into the net.
- Touches the net.
- Hits the ball outside the lines.
- Catches or gets hit by the ball.

So how do you achieve victory?
The first side to win six games
wins the set. To win the match,
you'll have to win two out of
three sets.

CHAPTER TWO

SMASH SESSION

You don't need a crown and a throne to rule the tennis court. You just need a racket, a tennis ball, and a wall to hit against. Even better, grab a friend and head to a tennis court at a local park. One of the coolest things about tennis is that it's a sport you can play with anyone.

Players warm up by rallying. They stand behind the baseline, smoothly striking through the ball after it bounces. Nailing groundstrokes—your forehand and backhand—is the key to a terrific tennis game. The more groundstrokes in a row you can hit, the more likely you'll win.

forehand

Forehand

A right-handed player uses a forehand groundstroke for shots that come to her right side. A left-handed player's forehand is on her left side. She grips her racket with one hand, swings it back, hits the ball and follows through. The racket ends up on the other side of her body.

Backhand

A backhand groundstroke is when the ball comes to a right-handed player's left side (again, it's reversed for a leftie). She goes through the same movements, but uses two hands instead of one.

backhand

11

Serving Starts It

All tennis games begin with a serve. The server stands behind the baseline and to the right of the hash mark. She gets two chances to get the ball in. Her goal is to get the ball cross-court into the service box, but keep it on or in front of the serviceline. She calls out the score, tosses the ball, and steps forward as she aims for an ace.

On her next serve, she goes through the same routine, but stands on the left side of the hash mark. She serves the whole game until one side wins. Then it's the other side's turn to serve.

After a serve, the server must quickly get ready for the next shot. A ball could come directly back to the server, so she must always be prepared. Tennis is a guessing game. Sometimes it's hard to tell where your opponent is going to hit the next shot. Think fast! You'll only have a split second to decide where you next want to hit the ball. A good strategy wins the match in tennis.

The Net Game

Sometimes players charge in and take control at the net. Here, players volley, which means punching the racket at the ball, rather than swinging at it. The ball pops back so quickly that the other player has to scramble to get it.

It's tough to get a ball past a player at the net. The other player may try to lob the ball high over her head. But if she doesn't get it high enough or far back enough, she's set herself up for trouble. The net player can move under the ball, swing her racket overhead, and hit the ball down. Smash!

"There's no one that I hate to play against. I consider everyone a challenge.

—Steffi Graf, former German tennis pro

CHAPTER THREE

GET IN THE GAME

To really reign at tennis, you have to play a lot of it! Hit more balls, play more matches, and you'll develop powerful strokes and strategies. Whether you win or lose, each new player you face will challenge your skills and smarts.

It's easy to find players to compete against. Just join a tennis club or league. Your town or your school may have a tennis team.

When you join, you'll drill to strengthen your strokes and play matches with teammates. Then, you and your teammates will play singles and doubles matches against other teams. If your team wins big, you'll all hit the road, traveling to state and sometimes regional and national tournaments.

But no matter how good your game is now, you can get better. If you're ready to get serious, consider taking private lessons.

Coaches can also provide you with top-of-the-line instruction and give you advice on your game and equipment.

The Mind Game

Tennis is a game of strategy. Does your opponent have a weak forehand or backhand? Guess what? If you hit more shots to her weaker side, she'll probably miss more shots! Does your opponent hit your powerful shots back even harder? Try hitting her a soft shot. You may catch her off guard.

Even as you study the other player, remember to play your game. If you have a solid forehand and backhand, focus on returning every ball. If you have a smash serve, perfect it until you can win a point with your serve alone. Love volleying? Get to the net. A tennis match is a chance to let your skills shine.

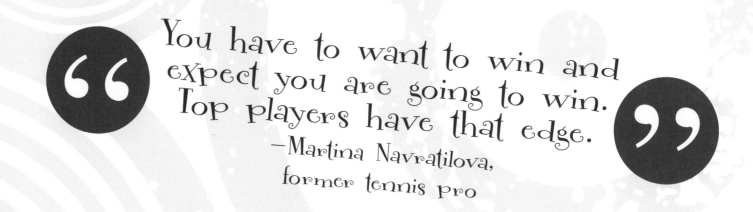

" You have to want to win and expect you are going to win. Top players have that edge.
—Martina Navratilova, former tennis pro "

CHAPTER FOUR

BECOMING A SMASH HIT

The best tennis players in the country strive to be ranked. They want to be part of the top 100 and eventually top 10. If you're serious about competitive tennis, the first step is to join the United States Tennis Association. Membership allows you to collect ranking points by playing in and winning matches in tournaments for your age group.

As you play and win, your ranking improves. You become eligible to play in more competitive tournaments and can win many more ranking points. Keep playing and moving up. Maybe someday you'll be number one!

Anna
Tatishvili,
junior pro player

Live Like a Champion

To become a champion, players have to eat, rest, train, practice, and compete like champions. Serious junior players eat healthy food and try to get plenty of sleep. Many practice from the time school gets out until dinner every day. Jogging is a good way to stay in shape and build endurance. Doing speed workouts develops the quickness that will come in handy on the court.

Some girls attend special tennis academies that offer both academic lessons and tennis lessons. They may study reading, writing, and math at the camp or at a local school until noon. Then they'll play tennis until 7:00 in the evening every day. Top junior players travel to tournaments almost every week, playing 60 to 100 matches a year.

Losers Are Winners

Did you know you have to lose to win? To improve, players must compete against better opponents. In fact, coaches expect players to lose one of every three matches.

Going Pro

Do you have your sights set on tennis gold? Maybe playing tennis in college is your dream. Many top-ranked girls win college scholarships. Or maybe you're looking at going all the way to the top and playing pro. Pros compete for big bucks on the Women's Tennis Association tour. To reach the top of the WTA, you have to give tennis your all. That means practicing all day, almost every day. You need endurance, agility, strength, and a winning strategy for every match.

A great tennis career is something that a 15-year-old normally doesn't have. I hope my example helps other teens believe they can accomplish things they never thought possible.
—Maria Sharapova, Russian pro tennis player

Maria
Sharapova

Getting to the Top

The best of the best strive to win a Grand Slam. That means winning the four most famous international tournaments: the U.S. Open, the Australian Open, the French Open, and Wimbledon. To win a Grand Slam in one year is an even greater accomplishment. Only five singles players in history have done this—and three of them are women.

CHAPTER FIVE

PRO PLAYERS

Do you have what it takes to go pro? Maybe you'll join these women whose hard work and dedication took them to the top.

When Althea Gibson was a kid living in Harlem, she won 10 national tennis tournaments. Back then, there were separate tournaments for black and white players. In 1950, Gibson became the first black player invited to play in the U.S. National Championships. In 1956, she became the first black player to win a major tennis tournament by winning the French Open. She then won Wimbledon and the U.S. National Championships. She integrated tennis for good when she won them both again the next year.

Althea Gibson

Billie Jean King

When she was 12, Billie Jean Moffit (later King) played tennis for the first time. "I knew that I would be number one in tennis," she says. She was right. King won 71 singles and 21 doubles titles, including a record 20 Wimbledon championships. She also played in the landmark Battle of the Sexes match in 1973, easily beating Bobby Riggs. "Be bold," says King. "If you're going to make an error, make a doozy, and don't be afraid to hit the ball."

Serena and Venus Williams

Imagine playing in the finals of one of the most important tennis tournaments in the world. Now imagine you get to play against your sister. That's what Venus and Serena Williams did–five times! Even though their competitive drive takes over when they are on the court, they remain good friends. Each sister has a long list of impressive victories. In 2000, Venus won the singles title at Wimbledon. Just one day later, the sisters won the doubles title. "Confidence is not something you can pull out of your tennis bag," the sisters say in their book, *How to Play Tennis*. "It's something you build with each shot you hit, each decision you make, and every game you play."

In August 1975, Martina Navratilova moved to the United States from Czechoslovakia to play tennis. But soon after arriving, she began gaining weight and losing matches. But she worked hard and got her body back in shape. By July of 1978, she was ranked number one in the world. During her career she won 167 singles titles, more than any other man or woman. Navratilova shares her winning strategy: "I think the key is for women not to set any limits."

Martina Navratilova

Now that you know all about tennis, grab a racket and a ball, and head out to the court! Remember, practice makes perfect, so get out there and play. Someday you just may be another Navratilova or Williams. The possibilities are endless.

GLOSSARY

backhand (BAK-hand)—a stroke made with both hands holding the racket; one arm starts across your body and the other arm starts out to the side.

forehand (FOR-hand)—a one-handed stroke made with the racket starting out to your side

groundstroke (GRAUND-strohk)—a shot made by hitting the ball after it bounces

rally (RAL-ee)—a set of shots hit back and forth until one player scores a point

tournament (TUR-nuh-muhnt)—a series of matches between several players, ending in one winner

volley (VOL-ee)—a shot made by hitting the ball over the net before it bounces

FAST FACTS

Tennis was popular with French medieval knights. Before serving they'd call out: *"Tenez"*, meaning "Here you are" or "Catch." In time, this service call became the name of the game: tennis.

Zero points in tennis is called "love." It's thought that "love" comes from the French word *l'oeuf*, which means egg, because a zero is shaped like an egg.

When you hit a tennis ball, it's in contact with the strings for only 4 milliseconds.

More than 80 percent of groundstrokes in top pro tennis bounce closer to the service line than the baseline.

READ MORE

Crossingham, John. *Tennis in Action.* Sports in Action. New York: Crabtree, 2002.

Wells, Donald. *For the Love of Tennis.* For the Love of Sports. New York: Weigl Publishers, 2006.

Williams, Venus, and Serena. *How to Play Tennis: Learn How to Play Tennis with the Williams Sisters.* New York: DK Publishing, 2004.

INTERNET SITES

FactHound offers a safe, fun way to find Internet sites related to this book. All of the sites on FactHound have been researched by our staff.

Here's how:

1. Visit *www.facthound.com*

2. Choose your grade level.

3. Type in this book ID **0736868259** for age-appropriate sites. You may also browse subjects by clicking on letters, or by clicking on pictures and words.

4. Click on the **Fetch It** button.

Facthound will fetch the best sites for you!

ABOUT THE AUTHOR

Elizabeth Rusch swatted tennis balls with a wooden Wilson racket from a very young age. She got serious about the sport her sophomore year at Guilford High School in Connecticut. On the girls' varsity team, she played both singles and doubles and went to the state tournament three times. She was also an assistant tennis instructor.

Now an award-winning freelance writer and author, Liz lives in Portland, Oregon, a half block from a public tennis court. She plays there with her husband and friends—and is teaching her two children the joys of tennis.

INDEX

backhand, 10, 11, 18

coaching, 17, 23

doubles, 6, 16, 27, 28

famous players,
   Evert, Chris, 4
   Gibson, Althea, 26
   King, Billie Jean, 4, 27
   Navratilova, Martina, 4, 29
   Williams, Serena, 28, 29
   Williams, Venus, 28, 29

fitness, 22
forehand, 10, 11, 18

groundstrokes, 10, 11, 16

ranking, 20

scholarships, 24
scoring, 8, 12
serving, 8, 12, 13, 18
singles, 4, 6, 16, 27, 28, 29
strategy, 13, 14, 16, 18, 24

tennis academies, 23
tennis clubs, 16
tennis courts, 4, 6, 8, 10, 22, 29
tennis history, 4, 26, 27, 28, 29
tournaments, 4, 16, 20, 23, 25, 26, 28

United States Tennis Association, 20, 24

Wimbledon, 4, 25, 26, 27, 28